MW01120866

ERIE CANAL SAL

**Wolcott Street School
Elementary Library Media
Center
LeRoy, New York 14482**

Copyright © 2010 by Gretchen Murray Sepik

This is a work of historical fiction. While some of the names, characters, places, and incidents are based on historical facts, others are either products of the author's imagination or, if real, used fictitiously.

All rights reserved. No part of this book may be reproduced or transmitted in any form or by any means, electronic or mechanical, including photocopying, recording, or by any information storage and retrieval system, without written permission from the author. Requests for permission should be addressed in writing to:
gmsepik@rochester.rr.com

Library of Congress Control Number: 2011902455
ISBN 978-0-615-44956-2
Published and printed in Rochester, NY.

This book has been published by Gretchen Murray Sepik, with the guidance of Betta Book Publishing. For more information, please visit www.BettaBookPublishing.com.

Publishing Guide, Editor: Kelly Sabetta
Author, Illustrator, Play Writer: Gretchen Murray Sepik
Cover Designer: John Neel
Photographer: Pat Mead
Printer: Book1One

This project was made possible, in part, with funds from the Decentralization Program, a re-grant program of the New York State Council on the Arts, administered by the Genesee-Orleans Regional Arts Council.

ERIE CANAL SAL

Wolcott Street School
Elementary Library Media
Center
LeRoy, New York 14482

WRITTEN AND ILLUSTRATED BY

GRETCHEN MURRAY SEPIK

There are various versions of some of the folktales found in this book. I have used 'Boaters and Broomsticks,' by Lionel Wyld, and published by North Country Books, Inc. in Utica; 'Low Bridge, Folklore and the Erie Canal,' by Lionel Wyld; 'Grandfather Stories,' by Samuel Hopkins Adams; 'Canal Boatman,' by Richard Garrity; and 'Mostly Canallers,' by Walter D. Edmonds.

There are a couple stories which I cannot locate the source for, so I have included a Bibliography in the back of the book. The Bibliography includes all of the books I used when originally researching and writing the script 21 years ago, as well as newer publications.

CONTENTS

Chapter | Page

ACKNOWLEDGMENTS

I would like to thank the following people for their help and contributions to this book:

Rose Gould Wentzel, for the idea of developing the character of a cook on the Erie Canal and her suggestion that I have the script adapted into a children's book.

My husband, Walter Jakubowski, for his encouragement and support which allowed me to get the project done, and for his assistance in scanning and touching up the artwork for this book.

My Mum and friend, Virginia Murray Sepik Kildoo, and my father, Michael Fredrick Sepik, for passing on to me the art of storytelling.

Special thanks to Orleans County Historian, C.W. Lattin, for his stories about his family and others in the county. Also, thanks to Sue Hurd from Hurd Orchards, for her stories about her family and farm.

Thanks to Megan Rosato, the narrator of the story, and her family, Kelly, Gregg, Brett, and Ollie.

A heartfelt thanks to my friends and neighbors who became characters in the story; Janice Ferris, Bill Lattin, Connie and Emily Mosher, Arthur Barnes, Dr. Jim Orr, and Emilio Dilodovico.

Thanks to Ed Smith, who provided a saying that his grandfather used to say to his father, "I'll give you the back of my hand as I have oft done in the past and as I am still well able to do, praise God!"

A thank you to my cousin, Marla Sepik, who, many years ago, replied to my question about why she had her foot up on the bleacher in front of us, “I’m discreetly picking at my toes in public.”

A big thank you to the Genesee-Orleans County Arts Council, who provided me with the grant money to get started on the project to adapt the script, ‘Surly Sal,’ into a book.

Thanks to the Master of Mural Mania, Mark DeCracker, who had Sal immortalized in a mural painted by James Zeger at the G. Winston Dobbins Memorial Park in the town of Lyons.

Thanks to Pat Mead, who has documented Erie Canal Sal’s visits to the Genesee Country Village and Museum with her wonderful photography and provided the photos which were used for the front and back cover design of the book.

Thanks to artist and photogapher, John Neel, for his guidance, expertise and design of the cover

Thank you to Young Audiences of Rochester and Young Audiences of Western New York in Buffalo, who have been placing Erie Canal Sal in the schools for the past 18 years, and to all the schools, churches, libraries, museums, historical societies, friends, and local citizens who have supported me through the years.

INTRODUCTION

'Erie Canal Sal' is historical fiction built around facts about the Erie Canal and is an adaptation of my original script, 'Surly Sal.' The performance piece and the book are funny from start to finish.

Years ago, I walked into a classroom to do storytelling. I had always loved storytelling and grew up in a family where both my mother and father incorporated it into our everyday lives as a teaching tool and as entertainment. Little did I know that the experience I had in that classroom, would determine the path my life would take.

I had gone to Point Park College in Pittsburgh, majoring in modern dance, minoring in acting, and taking writing courses. I eventually came to Rochester, and although I worked with the mime troupe, 'Flash in the Pan,' and became an apprentice with Garth Fagan's modern dance company, 'Bottom of the Bucket, but,' I was still nervous about speaking in front of a group of people. In order to present my stories, I developed the character Naomi Brown from the Blue Ridge Mountains, who lived in the early part of the 1800s. Naomi did the talking for me in a southern dialect, speaking of what life was like growing up in that part of the country and time period, and telling some of my favorite folktales from Joel Chandler Harris' stories of Brer Rabbit, Brer Bear, Brer Fox, and Miss Meadows and the gang. The program was developed to be interactive by using the children and teachers as part of the performance. Everyone in the audience was Naomi's children, and she would give them names and talk about their chores. Of course, the teachers were the ones caught napping in the hen house and picking their nose in front of the parson. I had a great time.

A short time later, a teacher requested a program using African Folktales, and the character Oganonda was born.

My husband suggested that I research the life of Mary Jemison and write a script, which I did. While presenting 'Mary Jemison,' at the Farmer's Museum in Cooperstown for the New York State Historical Association Conference, I met Rose Gould, a school teacher at Errick Road School in North Tonawanda. I began visiting her school to perform for the fourth grade students. Rose suggested that I do a program of an Erie Canal cook and gave me a copy of a section of a book that told about Old Black Nel, who was a cook on the canal in the early 1800s. She was described as being filthy dirty, and grouchy; both things I am very good at. I took this description and developed the woman Sal McMurray, who is filthy dirty, and grouchy - in a good hearted way; who is missing a front tooth, speaks in an Irish brogue, and loves to tell stories. I wove folktales throughout the script with facts about the canal.

I refer to my style of acting or storytelling as experiential theatre, because the audience becomes part of the program. In the case of 'Erie Canal Sal,' students sit close to me, and wherever I am telling the story, the audience is onboard a packet boat on the Erie Canal in the 1830s. Before I start a performance, whether it be in a school, museum, or library, I manage to get names of children or people in the audience, unbeknownst to them. These individuals become characters in the story; one becomes the captain, one crazy John, and one the widow. It is great fun to see the surprise on people's faces when I look dirctly at them and call them by name. Sometimes I even have personal tidbits that someone has shared with me about an audience member and that also gets included in the program. For instance, one of the audience members may have a dog named Buffy, or they like to sing. The program then becomes customized to the people who are there.

This style of performing is a great way to teach children about history, as they are now part of the experience, instead of just sitting and listening about it. My goal is to use every single child who is attending a program as part of the performance in one way or another. While performing 'Mary Jemison,' some the children are my brothers and sister, and I bring blankets to wrap them in. I also bring hats, necklaces, and shawls for them to wear, which draws them deeper into the narration. Some children have even asked me how I could still be alive after seeing 'Mary Jemison,' as they are convinced that I am the real Mary.

Sit back, relax, and enjoy a trip down the old Erie Canal with Erie Canal Sal.

For Walter and Mum

ERIE
CANAL
SAL

1

MEGAN HILL

Hello, my name is Megan Hill. Nice to meet you. Have I ever heard of Erie Canal Sal, you ask? Of course I have! Who hasn't? I first met her when my family was on it's way to Holley, New York, from Royalton, to live with my grandparents. My mother, brother, and I, got onboard a packet boat in Gasport. The boat was painted bright red and green, with a place to eat and a place to sleep as it hauled passengers. My father traveled by road with our dog Ollie, hauling some of our belongings in a wagon. The rest of our things were loaded onto a cargo boat on the Erie Canal to make the trip to our new home. I didn't know that the boat we had boarded was the very same boat on which Erie Canal Sal was the cook.

My brother, Brett, said Erie Canal Sal was a witch and he would tell me all kinds of stories about her; like how she could lift a mule with one arm, or how she could stand up to any man or woman in a fight. My brother even claimed that some folks say she kidnaps children and sells them to the gypsies; that she's part

Indian and can read people's minds, and she knows people's names before they tell them to her. She sure sounded like a witch to me.

Once we were onboard the boat, my brother, very matter-of-fact like, leaned over to me and said, "You do realize that Erie Canal Sal is the cook on this boat."

My brother is one to joke and I said I didn't even believe him one little bit. He then turned to some other boys sitting on the deck and asked who the cook was on the boat. The response was, "Erie Canal Sal."

I felt as though I had a case of the collywobbles and I put my hand up to my throat. I had been hearing about Sal for years and I thought that she was just someone that my brother had made up. And here I was sitting on the deck where she is reputed to have beaten up three men and booted them into the canal with the side of her foot. The same deck where some people say she turns into a cat at night, walks the tow rope to the shore, and prowls the woods.

My brother smiled at me. "You needn't worry. There's a way to find out if a person is a witch or a warlock. You just take a broom and lean it up against a wall. If a witch or warlock walks by, the broom will fall over, thus proving that the person is a witch or warlock," he said. He then stood up and walked to the other side of the deck returning with a broom, which he propped up against the side of the cabin and then sat down nearby smirking at me.

There we sat, waiting.

2

ERIE CANAL SAL

I was on the deck sitting on some crates with my brother, Brett, and some other children, when we heard this sound coming from down below where the bunks are located on the packet boat. It sounded like someone coming up the stairs, but there would be a heavy step, and then a pause, and then another step, and another pause, accompanied by grunting and huffing and puffing. A figure started to appear at the top of the stairs. It was an old woman and I have to tell you she was kind of scary. She had on a big, brown, wide-brimmed, felt hat with the front pinned up; a man's linen shirt with full sleeves, well worn and soiled; a faded black skirt, and a filthy, dirty apron. Hanging around her neck were two pouches tied with ribbon. They were some kind of potion. Her hair was a dark blonde, streaked with grey, and it hung down her back in a braid. She also had an earring that looped around the top of her right ear, which was very strange. She was carrying a large, black, cast iron pot, and when she finally reached the deck, she hobbled over to two crates; one stacked on top of the other, and set the pot down.

Unfortunately, she didn't pass anywhere near the broom, although I swear it trembled just the slightest bit when she came on deck. She then pulled up a stool next to the crates and took a seat.

Sitting next to me was a boy; I'd guess he was around my age, 10 years old. He was dressed like an orphan. His clothes were tattered and torn, and he had his shoes tied together with the laces, which were slung over his shoulder. He had red hair and freckles, and he just seemed to be smiling all the time, like he knew a secret that no one else knew. He leaned over and whispered, "Now that is where Sal holds court on fair days. Yes sirree, she don't like to be cooped up in the galley down below, so she brings her work on deck so's she can visit with folks that's on the boat. She cooks on that big cast iron stove over there on the deck when the weather is fine. I specks that's what she's planning on doing today, because you can see the smoke coming out of the stack. She do like to talk."

He winked at me and nodded toward Sal.

By then, a group of folks had started to gather. Some sat on chairs, benches, crates, and barrels that were on deck. Others were sitting on the roof of the boat with their legs dangling over the side. It was like they were gathering for a performance or a lecture. No one talked, they just sat and waited. Meanwhile, Sal just ignored the lot of us and sat there with her huge knife, cutting carrots into the black pot. Every once in a while, she'd look up and glance over the people sitting in front of her and then go back to her cutting. She did this several times, and each time, there would be a murmur that passed through the crowd. You could just feel the anticipation building up as though something big was going to happen. There were nervous giggles here and there, and then finally, she looks up and stares full at the group.

"What a fine lookin' boat load of people," she said in an Irish brogue. "Yes, yes, what a fine lookin' boatload of people," she repeated. "So well mannered and so clean," she said as her eyes swept over us and then lit on the young boy sitting next to me. "Most of ya," she said raising an eyebrow.

The boy chuckled and squirmed, obviously having a good time.

Another little girl sitting in front of Sal started to laugh, and Sal turned her attention to her and said, "What are you laughin' at?" The girl quickly covered her mouth trying to stifle her laughter. "I saw what you were doin' when I come onboard the boat and I got but one thing ta say to ya; there's no way ta be discreetly pickin' at yer toes in public." The little girl burst into laughter as did most of those on deck.

Sal turned back to the rest of us, placed her knife in the pot, and put her fists on her hips. "My name's Sal McMurray and I'm the cook on this here boat, so what I say goes," she said. "No cleanin' yer fingernails nor yer toenails with my forks, no spittin' on the floorboards, and no pickin' yer teeth with my knives, it dulls the blades." Her eyes swept over the group again and came to light on a boy, perhaps 13 years old, sitting in the back of the group. He was kind of slouching down like he didn't want to be seen. "And you," Sal shouted out pointing at him. "You think I don't remember you from the last time ya were onboard this boat? Well, I certainly do remember you and I would remind ya, no releavin' yerself from the top of the boat again." There was a great deal of laughter and the boy's face turned beet red, but he laughed, too.

"Yes Ma'am," he replied, as mannerly as you please.

Sal then bent over her task of cutting vegetables with the passengers anxiously waiting for what she might say next. "Now I don't mind talkin' while I work," she began. "Fact is, I like company while I work. My grandfather, Michael McMurray, used ta tell us that he supervised the diggin' of this here ditch. Well," she paused, "he was one ta stretch the blanket a bit, if ya know what I mean," and she winked at us. I had no idea what she meant.

The boy next to me shouted out, “It means stretching the truth.”

“It certainly does, John, but truth bein’ true, my grandfather did help ta dig this here canal of the State of New York and he used ta tell us wonderful stories late at night when we’d be in our bunks onboard my father’s cargo boat. He used ta tell us that the Irish contributed ta the buildin’ of this here ditch by workin’ as construction workers and diggers and stone masons, and along with their other fine attributes, they had a good sense of humor.” Sal then gave a great big smile and she was missing one of her front teeth. There was a big, black gap in her smile.

3

IT'S TRUE!

"Now, when they were buildin' the canal," Sal said, "they would put up these shacks fer the canal workers ta live in wherever they were workin'. The town's people all along the canal did not like the fightin' Irish, so one day some townspeople spread around a rumor that the Irish would get drunk and beat their wives. Well, the Irish heard about this rumor, this lie, and it made them mighty mad, so they planned a party come Sunday for the townspeople, because, ya see, on Sunday all the people would come out ta the canal ta see how the work was progressin'. So on this particular Sunday, when the Irish thought they had a big enough crowd gathered, all of a sudden out from these shacks came women, screamin' at the top of their lungs and flailin' their arms about, bein' pursued by their husbands with clubs in their hands. Their children put up a great uproar too. So the husbands chased the wives all through the crowd, and when they thought their act had lasted long enough, they went back into their shacks and laughed their full heads off."

At this, Sal burst into laughter, and laughed so hard her face turned red and her eyes watered, but hardly anyone in the audience laughed at all. She sort of hiccupped and wiped her eyes with the back of her hand, took out a huge, beige hankie from her bag, blew her nose very loudly, looked back and forth over the people seated in front of her, scowled, tucked her hankie into her bag, and went back to cutting vegetables. At this point, the whole crowd started laughing. Sal's head jerked up and she glared at us with her right eye squinting. "It's true," she said, making a big sweep with her knife from the right to the left and back again. "Can ya say that for me?" she asked us and then made another great sweep with her knife.

"It's true!" everyone said.

She nodded in approval. "I asked ya ta do that, because one time I was onboard the boat and I talked ta this boatload of people. I talked to 'em fer about two hours and not one of 'em said a word. Of course, I thought how well mannered they were. I found out later not one of 'em spoke English. I wanted ta make sure ya all spoke English so I don't sit up here talkin' ta myself." She gave that sweeping motion with her knife.

"It's true!" was the enthusiastic response from most of us.

4

REGARDING SNAKES

"Did ya know that the Irish are credited with gettin' rid of the snakes along the towpath of the Erie Canal, just like that saint in Ireland that got rid of the snakes? What was the name of the saint in Ireland that got rid of the snakes?" she asked.

"Saint Patrick," my brother called out.

"Very good," said Sal. "Saint Patrick. Are ya Irish?" she asked my brother.

"No," was his answer.

"Doesn't matter," Sal winked. "Yer smart and good lookin', anyway."

My brother nodded in agreement, and as Sal swept her knife back and forth the audience said, "It's true!"

Sal placed her knife in the pot and leaned forward, "Well now, the story goes like this. There was this packet boat captain and his name was Joe, and he picked up this boatload of Irish immigrants. As they were goin' down the canal, one of 'em was standin' on the bow of the boat watchin' the water go by when they come across a big school of water snakes. The immigrant leaned out a bit too far and he fell right inta the middle of this school of water snakes." With this, Sal screwed up her face and grimaced, then she continued. "This particular Irishman had not washed nor bathed since he left Ireland and all the snakes died from the poisonin'."

After much laughter from the passengers, Sal continued. "This gave Joe an idea. Ya see, when the Irish come over ta America, they'd bring with 'em a bowl of Irish field dirt, fer luck. So Joe went around ta all of the immigrants and took a handful of dirt from each of their bowls, and then as his boat was goin' down the canal, he would sprinkle that dirt along the banks. And since that time, there's hardly been seen a snake along the towpath." With this, Sal made a wriggling motion with her arm like a snake, and then picked up her knife and made that sweeping motion.

"It's true!" was the response.

Just then, the helmsman shouted out, "Low bridge, everybody down." The folks sitting on the roof of the boat bent down and we passed under the bridge at Middleport. This happened at each bridge we passed under, because some of the bridges are so low they could knock you right off the top of the boat. You have to squat down, lie down, or come down off the top of the boat, depending on the bridge you are going under and the boat you're riding on.

5

JACK MCCARTHY

The sun came out from behind a cloud and the day began to get warm. Sal put her knife down, unbuttoned her cuffs, and rolled up her sleeves. She was looking at me, then she picked up her knife and pointed at me. “Do ya know Jack McCarthy?”

“No,” I answered, happy to be included in the fun.

Sal was leaning on her pot, her lips pursed, and one eye squinting. “He’s lookin’ fer a wife.”

Everyone turned and looked at me, and I could feel my face blush red, but before I could say I was only 10 years old and not the least interested in getting married, Sal was telling about Jack.

“Strongest man on the Erie Canal,” she winked at me. “He’s a hoggee. Ya do know what a hoggee is, don’t ya?”

Some folks said, “No,” and some folks said, “Yes.” Sal pointed with her knife over towards the towpath.

“Now if ya look over there on the towpath, you’ll see the two mules that are pullin’ this boat. The man or boy that drives the mules is called a hoggee. ‘Ho,’ is the word they uses ta stop the mules, and 'Gee,' is the word they uses ta get the mules ta move. Our hoggee's name is Jim, if ya happen ta need ta know."

Sal picked up a potato and began to peel it, and then stopped abruptly. "Oh, I have ta tell ya this," she said excitedly with a big grin on her face. Once again, Sal placed her knife in the pot. She used her hands to paint pictures in the air as she talked. "One time we had a boatload of people onboard and they weren't nearly as well mannered as yerselves, and I says, 'Do ya know what a hoggee is?' This one young man, just as sassy as ya please, with his hands on his hips says, 'Of course we know what a hoggee is, we eats hoggees.' Well I shouted out ta Jim out on the towpath, I says, 'Jim, don't turn yer back on this group, they say they eats hoggees.' I just laughed and laughed and laughed," and Sal did just that; she laughed and laughed and laughed, and then she did a sweep of her knife.

"It's true!" we all laughed.

She sat there a minute staring into her pot like she was thinking, and then she asked the crowd, "Why were ya askin' me about hoggees?"

"We didn't," came the response from several people.

"Of course ya did, why else would I be talkin' about 'em?" she said, as she was glancing this way and that. She caught sight of me and said, "Oh, that's right! Yer lookin' fer a husband and I said I have just the man for ya, Jack McCarthy."

"I beg yer pardon," she said to the group, "I was the one who brought up the subject of hoggees," and then she turned her attention toward me. I had to laugh. She was so comical, and the way she would sweep her knife reminded me of the fairy godmother in a fairy tale casting a spell. She was not quite like I had imagined her.

"This is ta let ya know how strong Jack is. One night when he was takin' over his trick, he was hookin' up the mules when the mules broke the tow rope at the whippletree and ran off. This did not stop Jack; he picked up that tow rope, put it over his shoulder, and hauled that boat for-" she paused and held up three fingers, "five hours." My bother Brett tried to correct her about the number of fingers she held up, but she just kept on talking.

"The boat was a leaky old tub haulin' crushed stone, so it was sittin' low in the water, and as Jack was pullin' that boat the underside hit a large rock, ripped a hole right in the bottom, Jack kept on pullin'. The boat started takin' in water, and it got lower and lower and lower in the canal until it got inta the mud and got what we calls mud larked. Jack kept on pullin'. Luckily, the moon came out before he got ta the Genesee Aqueduct, because if he had tried ta pull that boat onto the aqueduct, he would have ripped the entire floor out of the aqueduct, and all the Erie Canal would have spilled right down inta the Genesee River. If ya don't know what an aqueduct is, it's a man-made waterway ta carry one body of water over another body of water."

Sal sat back nodding her head and squinting that right eye at the audience. Then she leaned forward. "He was pullin' west against the current, too. State legislatures voted ta award Jack $500.00 fer scoopin' the Erie Canal four feet deeper between Pittsford and Rochester."

We all laughed, and she did that thing with her knife and everyone said, "It's true!"

I was still smiling when she looked my way, and she said, pointing her knife at me, "Look at her smilin'. I could tell ya were a woman who likes a man with money." I covered my face with my hands, totally embarrassed. Sal started cutting carrots again. "There's nothin' wrong with that," she assured me with a nod, "I like my men with money, too."

She continued her tale about Jack. "Now Jack McCarthy is more nibble witted than most men I know, and he took that money and bought himself a pair of mules. Ya probably noticed that on the back of the boat there's a very foul smell." She pointed to the back row of men who were leaning against the cabin of the boat. The men shifted their feet and looked at one another as the rest of passengers turned to gaze at them. "No, no, no," said Sal. "It's not the men standin' there," she paused, "of course, I can't say that fer a fact, but on the other side of that wall toward the stern of the boat is where our stalls are, and that's where we keep our extra pair of mules, Paddy and Sean. When it comes time ta change the mules, we take the boat over ta the towpath and we puts down the hoss bridge. We calls it a hoss bridge, even though we got mules. We take off one pair of long eared robins. That's another name fer mules. Then we bring on the other pair of hay burners."

John, who was sitting next to me shouted out, "A hay burner can be a mule, or a horse, or an oxen, and, on a rare occasion, a donkey. Them's what folks use to pull their boats along the canal."

"You should know John," Sal said, wagging her knife at him and nodding. He was smiling from ear to ear and sat down glancing over at me, proud as could be. Sal continued. "It takes about 10 ta 20 minutes ta change yer mules, horses, or oxen, and an occasional donkey. It depends on the disposition of said mules, horses, oxen, or donkeys. So, Jack McCarthy trained his mules ta save his captain time." And with this, she held her knife in her left hand and walked the fingers of her right hand around the rim of the pot. "He trained 'em ta walk single file along the towrope like tightrope walkers."

Then she looked out at us with her lips closed tight, and that right eye squinting, and before anyone knew what they were doing, we all shouted out together, "It's true!"

She leaned back and chuckled, "Well, Jack McCarthy would have ya think so."

6

WALLY THE WONDERFUL

Sal then placed her knife into the pot and shuffled over to a huge black iron cook stove that was on the deck. She opened the door to reveal trays of biscuits that she removed and set out on a long table to cool. They smelled so good. She also set out a butter dish, knives, spoons, mugs, and some jam, jugs of milk and cider, sugar, and cream. On the stove there was a pot of coffee. Folks helped themselves to the biscuits and drink as she stoked the fire in the stove with the wood that was neatly stacked next to it. Once everyone had settled back into their places, she continued.

"My grandfather, Michael McMurray, come ta the states in 1819 from County Clare in Ireland, and as he was a fine stone mason, he started workin' on the canal. Then we come over in 1821. That was my father, Michael, my mother Virginia, and myself. I was then…" she stopped working and looked at a young girl sitting not far away and she asked her, "how old are you?"

"I'm 10 years old, Ma'am," the girl answered politely.

Sal continued, "I was 10 years old at the time." The girl smiled and scrunched up her shoulders in delight. I personally think that no matter what age the girl was, Sal would have said that was the age she was, just to make the girl feel good. If Sal was a witch, she certainly was an odd witch.

"Yes siree, we lived in shacks wherever my father and grandfather were workin' until the canal was completed." She stood up from placing wood into the cook stove; her face was red and drenched in sweat. She pulled out that huge, beige handkerchief from the leather bag she wore around her waist and wiped her face with it; and then, very noisily, blew her nose and stuffed it back into her bag. She made her way back to her throne, still talking. "What year was the Erie Canal completed?"

John jumped up, but she waved him back down. "Yes, John, I know ya know the answer, but let's give someone else a chance."

A man with a huge mustache said, "1825."

"The Erie Canal goes from where ta where?" she asked.

The same man answered, "From Buffalo to Albany."

She scrambled back onto her stool. "How many miles long is the Erie Canal?"

"It is 363 miles long," he shouted twirling his brown mustache between his fingers.

She picked up her knife and began to cut potatoes. "It's obvious ya been onboard the boat before," she glanced at him from under her eyebrows. "I'll have ta think of a hard question." Sal leaned back stroking her chin like she was thinking and then she got a big grin on her face. "Okay, I got a good one. As ya all know, New York State is not perfectly flat, so they had ta put these contraptions in the canal..." but before she could finish the sentence the man cupped his hands around his mouth.

"Locks! They put locks in the canal," he said confidently.

Sal scowled at the man. "I didn't even ask the question yet!" She then took a long look at the tall man sitting there on the crate, leaning against the wall of the cabin with his legs stretched out in front of him. You could tell he was smiling; not because you could see his mouth, because his lips were covered by that big, bushy mustache; but because the corners of his eyes were all wrinkled up. Then all of a sudden, Sal slapped her knee and threw her head back laughing. "Oh my word, if it isn't Wally the Wonderful. That's how he knew the next question I was gonna ask, he's a mind reader. I didn't recognize ya with all that hair on yer face. Take off yer hat." He obediently obeyed and his head sported a short crop of sandy blonde hair. "And ya cut yer hair. Why the last time he was onboard the boat his hair was so long it was clear down ta his behind." She was obviously excited and she held up her right hand. "Watch this, watch this," she said and then winked at us. "Wally the Wonderful, what am I thinkin' now?"

He didn't even pause, "There are 83 locks in the Erie Canal. They're like dams. They put a boat in between the two movable walls, close the walls, fills them up with water to raise the boat up to the rise of the land, or lets the water out to lower the boat down."

Sal grabbed her knife and with a sweeping motion she directed the passengers, "It's true!" they chorused.

"Indeed it is," she said. So this went on for a few more times of her asking Wally the Wonderful what she was thinking and him telling her. She was always tickled that he knew, but then all of a sudden he simply said he didn't know.

Sal had been very animated through all the asking and all the telling, but then she stopped and stared at him suspiciously with that right eye. She smirked, shook her head, and leaned back with both her hands on her thighs. "I know what yer tryin' ta pull," she said, bobbing her head up and down. She then turned her attention to us. “He did this ta me the last time he was onboard the boat. He was givin’ me one right answer after the other and then all of a sudden he says he can’t do it anymore. Of course if I was ta give him somethin’ ta eat and maybe some money, he’d be able ta give me some more right answers.” She then looked at Wally the Wonderful. “Well, I don’t need ta pay you ta tell me what I’m thinkin’, because I already know what I’m thinkin’, and I don’t need ta pay you ta tell me what I’m thinkin,” she said very fast. “But ya promised me that ya would tell me my fortune the next time ya were on the boat and I will pay ya fer that.” She glanced over at me and said, “I wanna know about men in my future,” and then she lifted up her shoulders and screwed her face up into a pleased expression. The people onboard chuckled because, not meaning to be disrespectful, she wasn’t very pretty; in fact one would have trouble imagining any man taking a liking to her.

7

CANNONS

Once again Sal took to cutting up vegetables into her pot. "Well, they opened the canal on October 25, 1825, and we were there. We were stayin' with friends in Gasport, and we got up early in the mornin' and went up ta the canal. The banks were just lined with people. We found a place ta sit and as we were sittin' there we heard a sound comin' from over towards Buffalo. It sounded like thunder."

"It was cannons!" I shouted out. I just couldn't contain myself. "My father, Greg, was manning the cannon in Gasport." I told her. I was very proud of the fact that my father was at the opening of the canal. I was there too, but I was only five years old, so there's not much I remember.

"Indeed, it was cannons," she said, "and isn't it funny that yer father's name is Greg. I've got a brother named Greg, too." I nodded in agreement. I glanced back at my mother who was sitting on a chair looking very pretty in her best dress and bonnet. She smiled, and I could tell she was enjoying all this storytelling and having a chance to just sit and watch the scenery go by with nothing to do and no one demanding her attention.

Sal continued, "They placed cannons all along the canal every 15 miles or so, and when the boats left Buffalo, they fired the first cannon, and then the men that were mannin' the next cannon fired theirs. The sound went the whole length of the canal, down the Hudson, and back again." She paused. "Only two men were killed." There was a gasp from some elderly women sitting nearby. Sal glanced over at them. "It happened in Weedsport. The men were lightin' the cannon and the cannon exploded. There were body parts, well, we don't need ta discuss that so close ta dinner." The ladies nodded in agreement. "We sat there a good part of the day, and then one young man, who was sittin' on the roof of the hotel, shouted out that the boats were comin', and sure enough there they were. Onboard the first boat was Dewitt Clinton himself. He was the governor of New York State responsible fer gettin' this big old ditch dug. Lots of folks didn't think the canal would succeed and they called it Clinton's Ditch or Clinton's Folly. They sure would have ta eat their hats fer sayin' such a thing once the canal was completed."

"Before he was governor, Dewitt Clinton was mayor of New York City," she added. "He had a barrel of water from Lake Erie that he was gonna dump into the harbor in New York City, and he called that, 'wedding of the waters.' Say, have any of ya met Dewitt Clinton?" she asked. A man in a tall, black silk hat touched his hat and Sal said, "Well of course Doctor Orr would have met him, he was his personal physician. The rest of ya are not gonna be able ta meet him because he has since crossed the dark river." Sal then bowed her head and crossed herself like Catholics do; you know, with her right hand touching her forehead, her chest, her left shoulder and then her right shoulder. I didn't know what she meant and I could tell other children on deck didn't know either, as they were looking at each other in a curious sort of way. Sal looked up and said, "So ya don't know what that means?" Several of us shook our heads. "Why it means he died."

She then continued. "The name of the first boat was the Seneca Chief, and behind his boat I counted 29 packet boats. There were steam boats, there were cargo boats, there was the boat haulin' Whitehall's Firemen, and onboard all those boats were hundreds of men and women dressed in their finest ta celebrate the openin' of the canal. DeWitt Clinton was standin' on the bow of the boat wavin' at people and my grandfather was sittin' next ta me on the bank. My grandfather stood up and took off his hat," Sal removed her floppy felt hat to reveal a somewhat untidy mass of graying hair that was pulled back into a long braid down her back, "and he shouted at DeWitt Clinton out there in the middle of the canal." She then pointed her finger at a boy and shouted in a deep voice, 'The mainstream of human progress is the itch in the restless man ta be otherwise than where he's at!' That means men likes ta travel. Listen ta this, listen ta this," she said excitedly, "DeWitt Clinton tipped his hat ta my grandfather," and with that she took hold of her knife, but before she could swish it, the crowd shouted out, "It's true!"

8

CRAZY JOHN

"Once the canal was completed," Sal went on, "my father and grandfather were out of work." Sal had her hat grasped in her left hand and was scratching at her head with her right hand, "But my mother made sure they had plenty ta do. She was tired of livin' in shacks and she wanted 'em ta build her a house. So they built her a house out of those stones ya find all in fields out around Lake Ontario and further out." Sal then picked something out of her hair, squished it between two fingernails, flicked it away, and then put her hat back onto her head. Yick! "What are those stones called?" she asked.

There was silence. Sal looked at some young children sitting to her left. "What does a turkey say?" she asked them.

"Gobble, gobble," they replied in unison.

"Now take one gobble and it rhymes with that," she said, sure they'd get the answer.

“Cobblestones,” the little boy said, quite pleased with himself.

“Yes, very good,” Sal said, “I got some in my soup pot.” She reached into her pot and started rummaging around. “I’m amazed at the number of people who don’t know what a cobblestone is,” she said.

She pulled out a potato as she continued to poke about in her pot and one of the boys said, “That’s a potato.”

Her head jerked up as she glared at him. “I know that’s a potato,” she said as she shook the potato at him. “If I didn’t know the difference between a potato,” and she held up the potato in one hand, “and a stone,” and she held up a cobblestone in her other hand, “ya wouldn’t wanna be eatin’ my food.” She then looked out at the rest of us. “They had famine in Ireland and my mother made stone soup, and ya can see I lived ta tell about it.” She turned to a group of young women who were sitting to her right. “I clean the stones real good before I puts ‘em in the soup pot.” She then wiped the stone with her filthy, dirty apron to make her point. There was a slight moan amongst the passengers.

She looked out at the young boy sitting next to me. “John, I feel I need ta remind ya about this. Don’t try ta eat the stones again.” This caused a great deal of laughter from the people, as well as John. “For those of you that don’t know, this is John. He used ta be hoggee fer our boat. He isn’t our hoggee any longer, but he is still a crew member. He trains all the hoggees we use on this boat and he trains hoggees used on other boats, as well. He is the most famous hoggee on the entire length of the Erie Canal. You all most surely have heard the song about John.” People looked at each other and shrugged their shoulders. Other people smirked as they obviously knew the song.

Sal looked over at John, “John, may I sing that song about you?” He nodded enthusiastically. Sal then explained to the passengers, “This is what we do when I sing John’s song. I start out with the chorus, and ya all listen, so the next time I sing the chorus, we can all sing it together. John likes ta come up and direct people when they're singin'. Sometimes he dances. I just never know what he's gonna do." She then looked at John. "Will ya come up and direct the people?"

He jumped up, leaving his shoes behind, and hurried to where Sal was sitting and stood there. Sal looked at him, and then reached out and gave him a little push. "I don't want ya standin' too close ta me John; ya sometimes gives me the willies." John stepped to the side a short distance from Sal, grinning broadly as she continued. "John, aren't ya trainin' another hoggee?" she asked; and she pointed to my brother, Brett. How she knew my brother was interested in working on the canal, I don't know, but it sent a chill up my spine that she seemed to know. My brother liked the animals on our farm and he liked riding the horses, but he wasn't much interested in farming. He wanted to travel to see the country, and the Erie Canal was a perfect place to start. My brother got up and stood on the other side of Sal. She cast a sidelong glance at him, "And what might yer name be?" she asked; but before he could answer she drew back in surprise and gasped putting her hand to her chest. "Oh my word, John," she said excitedly, as she turned toward John. "Isn't this Maddog Maloney?" John nodded in agreement. Sal stuck her hand out and shook hands with my brother. "Why, it is a great pleasure ta meet ya, Maddog. I've heard about yer exploits. I heard that ya can ride a horse and handle an axe better than most men twice yer age, and that ya have never backed down from a fight. That will surely come in handy on this boat, I can tell ya. Welcome ta the crew."

My brother looked very pleased with the fact that Sal had heard about his exploits and was using the name his friends had given him. Of course it all was in jest, because my brother was not

training to be a hoggee, but he went along with the fun. Still, it made me uncomfortable that she knew so much without anyone telling her. It gave me the creeps.

Sal faced the passengers again and began to sing in a low, throaty voice.

"John, John, crazy John.
Runs around with his long johns on.
Sometimes John puts his long johns on wrong.
Crazy John, Crazy John.

John, he was a big man.
Taller than any tree.
He was a mule skinner on the Ear-reye-eee.
Singin' hoggee, hoggee."

John stood on his toes as Sal motioned the audience, "Everyone!" and they joined in.

"John, John, crazy John.
Runs around with his long johns on.
Sometimes John puts his long johns on wrong.
Crazy John, Crazy John."

All the passengers joined in as John danced about and my brother directed the singing. What fun!

"One night poor John got kicked in the head.
Got kicked in the head
By a mule named Fred.
He lay so long we thought he was dead.
Poor John, poor John......and"

With this John fell, prostrate on the floor, as Sal and the passengers sang the chorus and my brother directed the singing.

"John, John, crazy John.
Runs around with his long johns on.
Sometimes John puts his long johns on wrong.
Crazy John, Crazy John.

Twas awhile before he came to.
He wandered around
Didn't know what to do.
Totally confused without a clue.
Poor John, poor John.....and"

John got up from the deck and staggered around aimlessly scratching his head.

"John, John, crazy John.
Runs around with his long johns on.
Sometimes John puts his long johns on wrong.
Crazy John, Crazy John."

John joined in on the last chorus, vigorously directing the passengers with great sweeps of his arms.

Sal leaned on her pot looking at all of us as she said, "Sometimes he puts the front in the back, and sometimes he puts the back in the front; and just so yer warned, they're bright red, and sometimes he runs around on the deck with 'em on his head."

Everyone laughed and clapped as John bowed, and he and my brother sat down. I leaned over to John when he sat down next to me and whispered, "Is that true?" just as Sal swung her great blade and everyone said very enthusiastically, "It's true!"

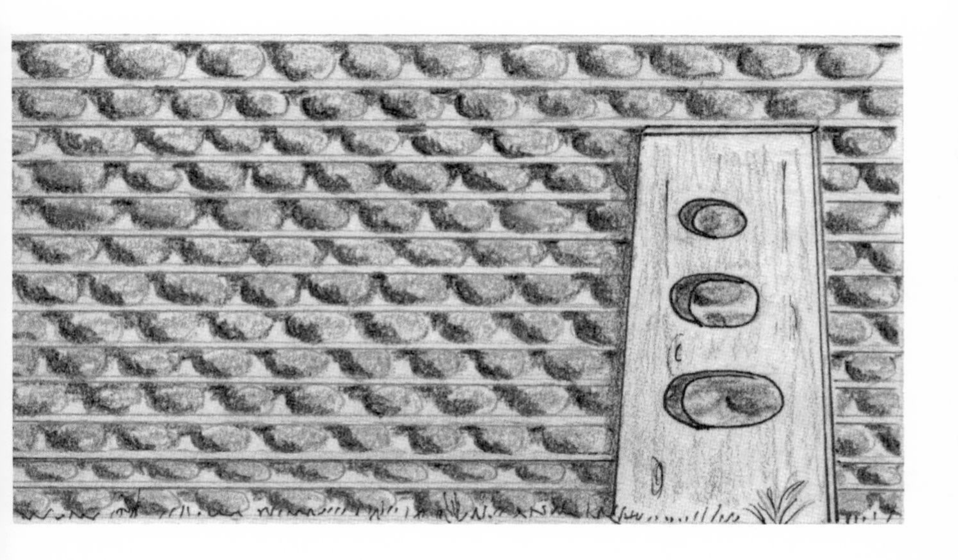

9

THE OUTHOUSE

Sal began cutting carrots as she spoke, "I helped ta build that house. I was just a child, but my father gave me a piece of wood with three holes cut out in the middle. I was ta measure the cobblestones and put them inta separate piles. The smallest cobblestones were fer the front of the house, the middle-sized cobblestones were fer the sides of the house, and the biggest cobblestones were fer the back of the house. It was the first job I had, and I made a penny a day. Faith, but didn't I feel rich as a pig in mud!"

"My father and grandfather fought the whole time they were buildin' that house. I remember on one occasion I was in the front of the house workin', and I heard my grandfather yellin' at my father. They were in the process of buildin' the privy, or outhouse, and I crept around the main structure of the house ta see what was happenin'. My grandfather and father were toe-ta-toe and nose-ta-nose, and my grandfather's face was beet red. 'I'll give ya the back of my hand as I have oft done in the past, and as I am still well able ta do, praise God. Only a waste-thrift would sand and plane the underside of a potty seat,' my grandfather said. A few days later, after the outhouse was completed, I went out and lifted up the potty seat, and the underside had not been planed nor smoothed."

Just then, the helmsman shouted out, "Low bridge, everybody down," as we passed under the bridge in Medina.

10

CARGO BOAT

"Once the house was completed, my father signed onto a cargo boat that hauled Medina sandstone," Sal continued, "and for the next few years, he went up and down the canal and he found himself to be a worthy canawler. He was tellin' my grandfather it was his greatest desire ta be captain onboard his own boat, so my grandfather went out and got him a boat. I'm ashamed ta tell ya how he got it." Sal shook her head, looked down into her pot, and paused until someone shouted out.

"He stole it!" Sal stiffened and scowled at the man who had made the remark, with that scary right eye, as she jabbed the blade of her knife in his direction.

"Of course he didn't steal it! What's the matter with ya? Everyone knows that stealin' is a mortal sin. My grandfather did not believe in stealin', he didn't believe in killin', nor drinkin', nor smokin', nor lyin'......much." There was a twitter of laughter, "But he gambled!" There was an intake of breath as the passengers seemed aghast at such a disclosure. "Just a wee bit, mind you, but he did gamble and he won this boat. We never thought it would float. It was in a sorry state. It was in a barn in dry-dock, which means it was up out of the water. My father and my grandfather were fine craftsmen, they worked on that boat during the off-season, and in the spring ya wouldn't have recognized it. They made it ta haul dry-goods, like wheat and meal, different kinds of spices, salt, sugar and such, and they named it, 'Jinny,' after my mum. Never was there born a sweeter woman than my mum," Sal smiled, as she remembered her mother.

"Now my father was from Ireland, and he was a common worker, a common laborer, but he come to America and now he was captain onboard his own boat. I remember the mornin' they launched that boat inta the canal, and my father walked onboard and stood at the bow of the boat. Oh, he was just as proud as a whitewashed pig. My mother went onboard, she was gonna be the cook, and my grandfather went onboard, and he did pretty much whatever he wanted ta do. I worked on the boat too, and my job was ta watch my younger brothers and sisters and make sure they didn't fall into the canal....too often." She peered out from under her eyebrows at us as she continued.

"So fer the next few years, we went up and down the canal, and our family kept on gettin' bigger and bigger and bigger until I had 13 brothers and sisters. Now I was 10 years older than my oldest brother, so I helped ta raise every one of 'em." She paused looking up. "That's what cured me of ever wantin' children of my own. That's true," she said, nodding.

Folks responded with a, "It's true!"

"Well of course it's true," Sal said. "I just told ya it's true." I clasped my hand over my mouth, because I had said, "It's true." I then realized that when Sal wanted the folks to say, "It's true," she would make a sweeping motion with her knife. That time she just nodded. I was determined I wouldn't shout out, "It's true," again until I saw the flash of her blade.

"How many of you have younger brothers and sisters that yer made responsible for?" Several hands shot up including my brother's hand. "Then ya know what a heavy cross it is ta bear ta have the responsibility of yer younger siblings placed on yer shoulders." My brother was sitting there, nodding in agreement with Sal. I stuck my tongue out at him. I know, not very ladylike, but you know how older brothers are.

Sal continued, "This is what I used ta do ta my younger brothers and sisters, and I did it to 'em fer their own good. I'd get a piece of rope, and one end of the rope I'd tie around the little one's waists, and the other end I would tie ta the hooks ya see on this side of the boat," she said, as she pointed to the side of the boat away from the towpath. "The length of the rope bein' such that if they did happen ta go over the side of the boat, they wouldn't quite hit the water."

With this description, Sal held two fingers downward and moved them quickly like one of her siblings kicking their legs. "If they weren't mindin' their manners, I'd get hold of the seat of their breeches and the rope, I'd hold 'em out over the water, and I'd give 'em a good shake. They'd mind their manners fer a good two weeks after that," she said, nodding her head and brandishing that knife.

"It's true!" we all shouted.

Sal continued to nod her head in agreement. "You can ask any one of 'em."

"Where are they?" a young man in the back asked.

Sal pointed to a pretty woman sitting on a keg behind the passengers pealing potatoes. "That's my youngest sister, Amelia Anastasia Wesley Leland Andrews Stockton McMurray. She has a long name because she was the last one born, and family members wanted their names passed on so she ended up with all the leftover names. She's onboard the boat learnin' how ta cook," Sal paused, "again." There was laughter and her sister just seemed to be ignoring her.

Sal looked at her sister and then gazed back at us. "I remember one time we were goin' under the Main Street bridge in Albion," she started. Anastasia looked at Sal with her eyes narrowed and her lips pursed. Sal ignored her displeasure and continued. "My sister was standin' on the top of the boat in the front, and when we came ta the bridge she squatted down. Once we were under the bridge she stood up, grabbed the underside of the bridge, and lifted her feet up, and the boat sailed right under her. She was of the mind that she was gonna drop down in the back of the boat. She didn't time it right," Sal chuckled. "I heard all this yellin' and screamin', and I turned around and there she was, hangin' from the underside of the Albion Main Street Bridge, her drawers blowin' in the breeze. What an embarrassment. The next boat had ta rescue her, and we picked her up in the next port." Sal shouted to her sister, "That was, what, two weeks ago?"

Her sister pretended not to be listening. Sal cackled as she swung her knife in that now familiar sweep.

"It's true!" we all responded, as we laughed.

11

THE LOCKPORT LOCKS

Sal pulled a huge, orange carrot out of her pot, "There were so many children onboard the boat that my mother decided ta stay behind at the house during the season, and my grandmother went onboard ta do the cookin' and keep an eye on my grandfather. I was of the age where I needed ta find a position fer myself, so I went to Mrs. Cashdollar's Cook's Academy for Bachelor Boaters, and I got myself a position onboard this boat where ya find yerself. Now, for those of you who cannot read, the name of the boat is 'The Saint Francis,' and when ya meet the captain, ya may address the captain as Captain Andrew Toon, or Father Andrew Toon. Why do ya think we call the captain, Father?" she asked.

"Because he's a priest," came the answer from an old man sitting in the back.

"That's right," said Sal pointing her knife in his direction, "he's a priest whose gone on the canal ta 'save souls!' as he would put it, and he is a mild mannered man, unless provoked ta the extreme. I remember one time we were in Lockport," she then paused and looked up from her carrot cutting. "Why's Lockport called Lockport?"

"Because there are lots of locks in Lockport," three children shouted, as they scrambled to their feet in excitement.

"Oh my word," said Sal, slapping her knee with her right hand. "You all should know because we picked ya up in Lockport. Let's ask the rest of passengers if they know how many locks are in Lockport." There was silence on deck, although the three children were fairly bursting, because they obviously knew the answer. Sal waited a few seconds, then repeated the question as she appeared to be brushing some hair from her face with her hand; and then she casually held up five fingers. Several of us caught onto what she was doing.

"Five locks!" we said in unison.

"Very good," said Sal, "it takes a long time ta get locked through five locks. In fact, these children told me they were walkin' along the towpath. Of course ya know yer not supposed ta be walkin' on the towpath, but, anyway, they were walkin' along the towpath and counted 123 boats waitin' in line ta get locked through the locks at Lockport. Imagine that, 123 boats!" Sal tilted and inclined her head slightly as she peered at us from under her brow.

"It's true!" everyone yelled, except me. Sal hadn't done that sweep with her knife.

She sat back on her stool and said, "I don't know if it's true or not, I wasn't there. Let's ask these three," and she pointed at the children.

"It's true!" they squealed, jumping up and down.

Sal swept her knife and we all joined in, "It's true!"

12

FATHER ANDREW

Just then, a fine looking man dressed in black, wearing a bowler hat, came and sat next to me, wiping his face with a large, red handkerchief. Sal brightened, "Faith, Father, weren't we just speakin' about yerself?" He smiled as he removed his hat and wiped the inside with his handkerchief.

"Were ya now?" he answered in an Irish brogue.

"Am I ta assume, Father," Sal continued, "that first mate, Mr. Barnes, is steerin' the boat?"

"Indeed he is, and a more able steersman you'll never find on the Erie Canal, as long as he keeps his mind on the tiller and not on drawin' pictures in that wee book he keeps in his pocket," answered Captain Andrew, as he leaned back against a keg.

"Well, Mr. Barnes is a fine hand at drawin' and paintin'," Sal said, "but, Father," Sal's voice was sweet as she addressed the captain. "Would ya mind if I told 'em about that big fight ya had in

Lockport?"

Father Andrew grinned, as he waved at her trying to put her off. "Please Father," she begged, as she leaned forward and some of the others onboard the boat chimed in as they obviously knew the story and wanted to hear it again. At that point, Father nodded and Sal sat back with a sigh.

"We were waitin' in line at Lockport ta get locked through," Sal started. "I don't know how many boats were in line, because I was down below makin' Father's favorite pie, when I heard a commotion. Well, what happened is this. The boat behind us, the 'Try and Catch Me,' had come right up so close that it was almost touchin' our boat. Words were exchanged between the crew of our boat and crew of the 'Try and Catch Me,' and words changed ta action in the form of fists." With this, Sal held up both her fists.

"I came up on deck just then ta see what was goin' on and I saw that three of the crew of the 'Try and Catch Me' had Father down on the deck. Luckily, I had with me my rollin' pin." She pulled out from under her stool a large rolling pin. "I call her Old Nell, and I hit two of 'em and booted them into the canal. The other man swung around, and his fist caught my cheek, my head hit the side of cabin, and I lost a tooth." She curled her lips up to reveal a space where one of her front teeth was gone. "Ya probably didn't notice I am missin' a tooth." We couldn't help but notice! She continued, "Father Andrew had by then gotten up, grabbed that man by the scruff of the neck, and picked him clean off the deck. 'That's no way ta treat a lady,' he said. He drew back his fist and he hit that man, I decked 'em and we booted 'em into the canal."

The entire deck was cheering and clapping as they strained their necks to see the captain. He was so good natured about it all. He stood up and took a bow and then sat down again as Sal's knife cut the air. "It's true!" was the consensus.

"About two weeks later, Father was givin' this sermon about

bein' forgivin' and turnin' the other cheek," Sal said, putting her hands together in a praying position and looking up at the sky in mock humility. "Faith, wasn't I confused, so I went up ta Father after the sermon and I said, 'Father, I don't understand this business of turnin' the other cheek and bein' forgivin' because, ya know, two weeks ago that man hit me and then you hit him. How is that turnin' the other cheek?' Father replied, 'Well darlin', the way I sees it, he hit you in your left cheek, and I hit him in his right cheek, so I did, indeed, turn the other cheek,' and then he crossed himself," which Sal demonstrated.

Again the passengers laughed, clapped, and cheered, and Father stood up, yet another time, and took a bow. Sal, using her knife like a conductor in front of a band, inspired us to shout, "It's true!"

13

FARMER DILODOVICO

"I know Father is here ta make me hurry along with my cookin'. Yer probably wonderin' what I'm makin'," Sal said, still cutting carrots as she nodded towards her pot. "I'm makin' poor man's soup, and the reason I call it poor man's soup, is because this mornin' I was buyin' vegetables from Farmer Dilodovico," she paused. "Ya see, some of the farmers come right out inta the canal in their boats, and we buy things from them. I always buy from Farmer Dilodovico. I was on the deck here talkin' ta a couple of young women who want ta be cooks, and I've taken on the burden of trainin' 'em." Sal glanced to the side at a couple of nice looking women sitting next to her sister, both cutting vegetables and looking embarrassed. Sal then leaned forward toward us. "Ya probably know about the accident that farmer Dilodovico had with the pitchfork, the pig, and the potato." She scanned the group, but no one seemed to have heard about the accident, but there was an excited murmur about wanting to hear the full story. "I'm not gonna tell ya the whole story, suffice it ta say he's missin' an eye." This caused a disgusted moan to erupt from the group.

"He wears an eye patch," she said, as she covered her right eye with her hand. "So, I was tellin' these young women about how ta buy from the farmers, and didn't realize we were so close ta Farmer Dilodovico's farm, when one of 'em grabbed my arm and pointed down toward the water at the back of the boat. 'Look Sal,' she said, 'pirates!' I hurried over and looked, and there was Farmer Dilodovico in his boat. I laughed so hard it's a wonder I didn't hurt myself. Imagine that, pirates on the Erie Canal." She chuckled loudly, as she swung that metal knife.

"It's true!" we all parroted.

"We bought parsley, eggs, milk, honey, broccoli," she said, as she rooted around in her pot, "potatoes," she said holding up a potato, "onions, and carrots," displaying each item.

All of a sudden, she gave a gasp as she caught hold of something, and slowly lifted it out of the pot. It was a long, dark, thin, ropey thing, and someone in the back shouted, "It's a rat!"

"A rat?" Sal repeated in disbelief. "I wouldn't be puttin' a rat in my soup," she paused, "not intentionally. It's a beet." And with that, she pulled the rest of the "tail" out of the pot, and there at the end was a beet. I have to admit, it did look like a rat tail. "I don't like beets in my soup," she said screwing up her face. And with that, she set the beet aside. "I don't know who put it in there," she said, looking straight at my brother, Brett.

He threw his hands up, "It wasn't me," he said.

"Are ya sure?" Sal asked, squinting that right eye and tilting her head.

"It's true!" he said, which caused an eruption of laughter on deck.

"Anyway," she continued, "my point is that Farmer Dilodovico had no meat fer me ta buy, so that's why I call it poor man's soup. Now, if Jim out there on the towpath, our hoggee, finds a woodchuck, a rabbit, a squirrel, or such, then we'll have rich man's soup, because we will have meat ta put in it. If the woodchuck, or squirrel, or rabbit has been lyin' around dead for awhile, then we'll have rich man's stew."

There was a groan from the passengers. Sal wagged her knife in the direction of the two young women who were learning to cook. "Remember this, young women; the longer the meat lies around, the more tender it becomes, and it makes a nice, thick gravy. Ya have ta add a few more extra herbs, but it's well worth it. Isn't it Father?" she asked, turning to Father Andrew.

He nodded, "Sure it is darlin'. I ate six bowls last time ya made it." Then he swung his arms and the passengers laughed as they said, "It's true!"

14

PATHMASTER LATTIN

Sal's attention was drawn to the towpath, where a tall, lean man was striding along at a great clip, with a walking stick in his hand. Sal gave a shout and the man's head jerked, as though awakened from a daydream. Sal waved, and he responded with a huge smile and a shaking of his stick. "That's Pathmaster Lattin, he's a canal walker," Sal told us. "We grew up together and my family used ta call him the Pieman, because he had an uncanny way of knowin' when my mother was bakin' pies. I recall on one occasion, mother was bakin' pies fer Christmas, and he came in the back door, crawled on his hands and knees until he was kneelin' in front of my mother with his hands clasped, and begged her fer a pie. My mother laughed so hard that tears ran down her face. She then gave him a pie forgettin' that she had just given him one the day before." Sal gave a chuckle remembering the event. "He walks this section of the canal makin' sure everything is in good repair. In fact, this is where there was a breach or break in the canal a few years back. The water roared down Beardsley Creek and swept Mr. Bullard's henhouse right off of it's foundation with hisself and his daughter inside, along with the chickens. His daughter jumped out where Beardsley Creek crosses Gaines Basin Road and Mr. Bullard exited the henhouse when it crashed into a tree. Mr. Bullard and all of the chickens were safe after their ordeal." We all gave a sigh of relief, but Sal continued, "Although the chickens wouldn't lay any eggs fer a week." Sal brandished her knife and the group sang out, "It's true!"

Sal continued as she cut some potatoes, "Now here ta the north, in that brick house, is where Pathmaster Lattin lives, and there was another breach in the canal right here and two boats were washed up on to Mr. Lattin's front yard. They got the boats back inta the canal by greasin' the skids with homemade soap made by Grandmother Lattin. If ya asked Pathmaster Lattin, he'll tell ya," and before Sal could finish her sentence the crowd shouted, "It's true!" Sal nodded with approval. It was as though we had gotten into a rhythm, anticipating her directing; or was she using magic to make us respond?

The helmsman then cried out, "Low bridge, everybody down," as we passed under the Main Street bridge in Albion. We docked there a short time to take on passengers.

15

THE WIDOW FERRIS

Sal, still cutting up her vegetables, swept her eyes across the passengers, to see who had gotten onboard at Albion. Her eyes settled on an attractive, older woman, quite fashionably dressed, seated on a bench in the back. "Oh my word," said Sal, "it's Mrs. Ferris. I'm so sorry ta hear about yer husband, God bless his soul," Sal said, bowing her head and crossing herself. She was silent for a moment and then became animated again. "But it's a wonderful thing ya did with all his money, buildin' that orphan's asylum in Albion." Sal then turned to me. "Ya see, Mrs. Ferris prefers her men with money too, and she does wonderful things with the money." Sal turned back to Mrs. Ferris. "I beg yer pardon, Mrs. Ferris, may I be so bold? Was that yer sixth or seventh husband?"

"It was my seventh husband," Mrs. Ferris answered quite proudly.

Sal looked at me again. "Mrs. Ferris built the orphan's asylum, the church, and a school for young girls." She turned back to Mrs. Ferris. "I hear that ya might be buildin' a library. Is that true?"

Along with everyone else on deck, Mrs. Ferris said, "It's true!"

16

CONSTANCE MOSHER

Several more people came onboard, and Sal caught sight of a little girl carrying a bundle in her arms and wearing a straw hat. She sat right in front of Sal and seemed not to be the least bit concerned with the big knife Sal was wielding, or the fact that Sal might be a witch. Perhaps she didn't know. Sal squinted her eye and looked at the child closely. "Ya know who you remind me of?" The little girl smiled and hugged her bundle tighter as she shook her head no. "Constance Mosher. Do ya know Constance Mosher?" she asked the child, as she picked up another carrot and started cutting.

The little girls eyes lit up. "Yes, that's my mother."

"Ya don't say?" Sal said, leaning over her pot and taking a closer look at the child. "And what might yer name be?"

"Emily. Emily Mosher, Ma'am," she said.

“Is yer mother onboard the boat with ya?” Sal asked, glancing around at all the faces.

“No, I’m traveling with my Aunt Gertrude,” the little girl replied.

Sal leaned back on her stool, and we all knew that another story was about to commence. “I met yer mother in New York City when she had just married yer father. Yer father was a packet boat captain and yer mother was gonna be the cook onboard his boat.” With this statement Sal gave a great, “Ha! With her cookin’,” and then she continued, “yer father’s boat was in Buffalo in dry dock bein’ repaired, so yer father and mother were gonna travel with us up the Hudson River and across the state ta Buffalo. The first mornin’ yer mother got up and I had laid out this table. I had fish I’d caught on the over-night trowel line. I think it was bass and pike. Bacon, steak, sausages, ham, a big platter of scrambled eggs, boiled potatoes, white bread, wheat bread, corn bread, fresh butter, buckwheat pancakes, wheat pancakes, with maple syrup, sourgum, and honey ta taste, oatmeal, and ta wash it all down, there was coffee, cider, tea, milk, and skimigig. ”

“What’s skimigig?” I asked, having never heard the term before.

Sal scowled at me, “It’s a fermented type of drink, and in my opinion, it is as bad as drinkin’ liquor,” she answered. “And as ya all know, drinkin’ is a mortal sin,” she shouted shaking her knife up in the air, “but some of the men who come onboard the boat have ta have their skimigig. I don’t approve of it nor does Father Andrew.” Father Andrew nodded.

“Anyway, yer mother come on deck dressed in her weddin’ dress. It was a beautiful teal-green silk basque, or jacket, lined in satin, with a flowing skirt ta match, a hat with feathers and silk flowers, and a parasol ta protect her from the sun. She was very dignified and refined, and just the prettiest thing, just like you,” she nodded at the little girl. Sal then imitated a stately woman with her parasol over her head, swinging her shoulders as though she were walking. We all laughed; she was so comical. "Well, yer mother saw the table with all the victuals, and she calls ta me in a most ladylike manner."

Sal's voice took on a high pitched, refined quality, as she imitated Constance Mosher. "'Cook, oh cook, you don't always prepare this much food all the time do you?' I said, 'Of course I do,' in an annoyed tone. Well, yer mother took me aside and she said, 'I'm supposed to be cook onboard my husband's boat and I can't even boil a potato.' And with this confession, she gave a long liltin' laugh." Sal threw her head back and gave a melodious titter.

"'Well', says I, 'it's never too late ta learn,' and as I had another apron onboard the boat, I puts it on her, and she helped me cook from New York City the whole way ta Buffalo. By the time we got ta Buffalo," Sal paused, as she speared a whole potato in her pot and lifted it up in the air on the end of her knife, "she could do more than boil a potato; she could burn one too!" This caused the newcomers to laugh, because they obviously knew the little girl's mother.

And before Sal could take the potato off her knife, the crowd had shouted, "It's true!"

Sal cocked her head to one side as she looked at the little girl, "Has yer mother's cookin' improved?"

Emily smiled broadly and said, "Yes, she's one of the best cooks in the town of Albion. In fact, folks come to our house on Thursday nights for prayer meeting with my father and dinner afterwards, and they say my mother is the best cook in all of Orleans County."

"I taught her everything she knows," was Sal's response.

"I know," Emily replied. "My mother told me to give you this," and she handed Sal a piece of paper. Sal looked it over and then laughed.

"It's a recipe," she told us, "a recipe for Aunt Constance's Poor Man's Soup with the last ingredient being one well-washed cobblestone."

"It's true," Emily added to the delight of passengers.

AUNT CONSTANCE'S POOR MAN'S SOUP

Sautee:	Oil	1 Tbsp.	Thyme	1/2 Tbsp.
	Onion	1	Parsley	1 Tbsp.
	Garlic	1 Clove	Pepper	3/4 Tsp.
	Celery	3 Stalks	Salt	1 Tsp.
	Basil	1 Tbsp.		

Add:	Water	3 Quarts	Cook 20 Minutes
	Barley	1 Cup	

Add:	Carrots	2 Cups	Miscellaneous	1 Cup
	Potatoes	2 Cups	Peas	1/2 Cup
	Tomatoes	2 Cups	Corn	1/2 Cup

Optional: One, very clean, lake washed, cobblestone.
Simmer for one hour.

17

THE SKUNK

"Well," said Sal, standing up, "I got ta go finish this soup." We all groaned, disappointmented that she was done telling stories. She stopped, put her pot on the crates, sat back down on the stool, and began cutting vegetables again. "All right, one more story. Are there any Italians onboard the boat?" Before anyone could respond, she started telling the next story. "We picked up a boatload of Italian immigrants in Albany. They had just come over the ocean from Italy, and they had been eatin' pasta the whole way and they were starved fer meat. Every time one of 'em would see a woodchuck along the towpath, they would get off the boat and try ta catch it. Apparently they don't have skunks in Italy, because the helmsman shouted out that there was a black and white woodchuck over in that field. Twelve of the Italian immigrants got off the boat and surrounded that black and white woodchuck, and it sprayed every one of 'em. That didn't stop 'em. They killed that black and white woodchuck and made a stew. One man told me it was the best woodchuck stew he ever had." With this, Sal wrinkled up her nose. "When it come time ta change the mules, the mules on the towpath refused ta get onboard the boat because of the smell. We had ta use the same pair of mules the whole way ta Buffalo. When we got ta Buffalo the Italians got off, but they left behind that smell. We couldn't haul passengers fer two weeks. In fact, yer the first group ta come onboard the boat and not notice the smell."

There was a lot of laughter in the crowd, and before Sal could send her knife sweeping, a heavy set man with thick, black hair and a full beard said, "It's true! We have no skunks in Italy."

Sal responded, "And there ya have it."

18

THE FROG

Just then, Sal caught sight of my new shoes. "What pretty shoes. Are they new?" she asked.

"Yes," I answered, looking down at my new, shiny shoes.

"I got new shoes, too," said Sal, as she held up her feet. The shoes were dirty and well worn. Sal continued, "I got 'em off a dead woman along the canal," and then Sal crossed herself; "God bless her soul," she said.

This caused a reaction from the passengers. People were disgusted that she would take the shoes off of a dead person.

"I knew her personally, and I knew she would want me ta have 'em, as she was no longer needin' 'em; and I was in need, but let this be a lesson to ya. She died of drinkin' too much liquor. And as ya all know, drinkin' is a mortal sin!" she shouted.

"But there's a problem with the shoes. Ya see, the right shoe has a heel and the left shoe does not, because her right leg was shorter than her left leg, which is a problem for me, because my left leg is longer than my right leg. But they're better than the ones I had before, as there are no holes in the bottom." She held her feet up high enough for us to see the bottom of the shoes and there were no holes.

She swept her knife across the air. "It's true," we said.

People began making suggestions about how she could fix the shoes, and I began to go over in my mind what she had said. I realized that she had made a joke at our expense, for she had simply said the same thing two different ways. I put my hands on my hips and I gave her a look, and she knew I was the only one onboard the boat to get her little joke. She winked at me and laughed loudly.

"Tomorrow, after breakfast, we're gonna have races," Sal said, as the boys sitting around the deck whistled and cheered. "Races between bedbugs, cockroaches, or fleas; it depends on what ya find in yer bunks tonight." This caused a great moan to erupt from the crowd.

Sal chuckled, as she asked a little boy in the back what his name was. He had long, blonde hair and was just as cute as could be. "Jason," was his answer.

Sal's face lit up. "Jason, why I know a story about a frog named Jason." This obviously pleased the little boy very much. "Watch fer frogs along the banks, and we'll have a frog jumpin' contest tomorrow." Some of the boys immediately went over to the side of the boat to look into the water, as though they might jump into the canal just to get a frog. Boys!? "I'll tell ya the story, then I have ta get on with my cookin'. I get ta talkin', and then I don't work as fast as I could, or should, or would, if I wasn't talkin'." She tucked her knife into the leather bag that she carried around her waist and placed her hands on the edge of her pot.

"There once was a frog, and his name was Jason, and he started his life in the Erie Canal as a tadpole," with this, Sal waved her hand in front of herself like a tadpole swimming. "Jason ended up in a pond in Brockport, where he kept on gettin' bigger, and bigger, and bigger, until his hind legs were six feet long. Locals used Jason ta help them haul the wood that was too heavy fer the horses," she continued.

"One day there was an emergency. There was a hill in Brockport; it was a little hill, as hills go, but in Brockport it was considered a big hill, because most of the land in Brockport is so flat. The name of the hill was Snake Hill, and goin' up Snake Hill there was a road, and the road went like this," Sal swept her arm around like a snake slithering. "The road was called Snake Hill Road, so they went up ta Jason the frog, who was nappin' next ta the pond, and they woke him up and asked him if he would help. Now, Jason was a bit cranky havin' been just woke up from his afternoon nap." Sal stopped her story and asked Jason, "Jason, do ya ever get grouchy?" Jason looked at his father sitting next to him, and his father gave a very vigorous nod of his head and Jason grinned wide. "I think we all get grouchy from time ta time. Myself more than not," confided Sal, "as my sister can attest to." Her sister rolled her eyes and nodded more vigorously than Jason's father.

"Anyway, Jason was in a bit of a grump, and he got hisself all puffed up." Sal puffed her face up and filled her cheeks with air. She looked very funny. "And then Jason the frong says, 'Ribbit, ribbit.'" Sal made the most realistic sounding frog I have ever heard. There was lots of laughter at her comical antic. "So they hooked a chain around Jason's neck, and the other end they attached ta the road, Jason gave a heave and straightened that road right out." With this, Sal spread both her arms wide, bowed her head, and the entire crowd shouted out, "It's true!" Everyone except John and me, because she didn't make that sweeping motion with her knife.

Sal's head shot up and she placed her hands on her hips. "Of course it's not true!" she said. "That's a tall tale. If ya don't know what's true and what's not true on the canal, yer gonna get takin' advantage of. Isn't that true, Jason?"

"It's true," agreed Jason, to a burst of laughter and applause from those on deck.

Just then, the helmsman called out, "Low bridge, everybody down," as we went under the bridge in Holley.

19

GARLIC

Sal stood up, "I've got ta go and finish this soup." She paused, looking at a small, pretty woman, plainly dressed, seated on a crate. "Ya know," Sal said to the woman, "I couldn't help but notice that ya got the same problem I used ta have. Do ya know what I'm speakin' of?"

The young woman said, "No, I'm sure I don't."

"Men!" Sal said, very forcefully shaking her fist. "I could see the men watchin' ya ever since ya come onboard the boat. I tell you it is a burden bein' pleasin' ta men. I should know; men used ta flock ta me like bees flock ta honey." As Sal spoke, she strode back and forth across the deck gesturing with her arms. "I had ta go ta that Gypsy woman up north of Albion ta get a potion ta keep the men away, or I would never get any work done. I always keep extras onboard the boat, and I would like ta give ya one so ya can enjoy the rest of the trip." With this, she removed one of the pouches that she had hanging around her neck. "I have ta make sure that it's still potent, I need a young man ta smell it." My brother, Brett, volunteered. She held the pouch up to his nose. He gave a big sniff and then he groaned, turned his face away in disgust, and held his nose.

"Good, good," said Sal, "it's still potent." She went over and handed it to the young woman. Sal then bent down, and said in a low voice, "It'll help that other little problem ya been havin', too." She winked at the woman, and the woman sniffed the pouch, and then held it away from herself. "Yes," said Sal, her hands on her waist, "garlic is a wonderful herb. If ya wear it raw, it repels the men; if ya cook the garlic, it attracts the men. It's true!"

20

GRANDMA AND GRANDPA HURD'S MULE BARN

With that, Sal picked up her black, cast-iron pot, waved her hand, and was turning to go when she shouted, and pointed to the north side of the canal. "Look Megan and Brett, there's yer Grandfather Hurd in front of his mule barn hookin' up mules ta that boat." We ran to the railing, and sure enough, there was grandfather, with his long, white hair hanging down past his collar, and his broad-brimmed hat shading his face.

"Grandfather, Grandfather!" we both called out. He looked up and waved. He shouted something, but it was carried away by the wind. We would see him soon enough, as we were disembarking at the bridge at Bennets Corners.

Sal offered up yet another story. "See that little house just east of yer grandfather's mule barn? That's where Kate Lavender used ta live. She had been a cook on a cargo boat on the canal, and took ta workin' fer yer grandmother. Yer grandmother told the story that one day Mrs. Lavender walked over ta her house and said she had somethin' fer her as a weddin' gift. Now, Mrs. Lavender was not much ta look at, nor one fer many words, and yer grandmother wondered what she could possibly have ta give her. Yer grandmother, bein' a proper lady, carefully followed Mrs. Lavender over ta her small house, avoidin' the patches of mud in the path. In the kitchen was a large barrel with the top removed, and it was full of packin' straw. In the straw, very carefully stowed, was some fine, blue china. Mrs. Lavender carefully counted out four bowls, four plates, four cups and saucers, a serving bowl, platter, creamer, a sugar bowl, and a gravy boat."

"'There,' she says, 'you'll have that and no more.' Yer grandmother confided in me that she wondered what else might have been hidden in the straw in that barrel."

Sal then picked up her pot and made her way to the door that led below deck. She walked past the broom, and the broom began to tip toward her like it was going to fall; but Sal stopped, looked at the broom, and it settled itself back against the side of the cabin, almost like it was alive. Sal then turned and looked straight at me with that squinty, right eye, smirked, and said, "A new broom sweeps clean, but the old broom knows the corners." She then disappeared down the steps and into the gloom below, chuckling.

I never did get to sample any of Sal's soup, because our stop was the next one, and we left the boat and were greeted by my grandparents.

We work on my grandparent's farm planting apple trees, peach trees, and cherry trees, as well as harvesting the fruit. My family lives in the same little house that Mrs. Lavender lived in, and my father and mother have fixed it up just fine. We are right on the canal. Our dog, Ollie, knows the sound of Sal's boat. She barks to be let out of the house when she hears it coming along the canal, because Sal always saves a bone or two, and heaves them over to the shore for Ollie. We wave, and I'm reminded of my trip on the Erie Canal with Erie Canal Sal and her tall tales. Just the thought makes me smile and sometimes laugh outright.

I tell you, on windy, winter nights, when the canal is closed for the season, I sometimes wake and swear that I hear the haunting sound of Erie Canal Sal laughing.

It's true!

BIBLIOGRAPHY - PRIMARY

Harness, Cheryl. *Amazing Impossible Erie Canal*. New York: Aladdin Paperbacks, 1999.

Spier, Peter. *The Erie Canal*. Utica: North Country Books, 1999.

Andrist, Ralph. *Erie Canal*. New York: American Heritage Publishing Co., 1988.

Hilts, Len. *Timmy O'Dowd and the Big Ditch*. San Diego: Harcourt Brace Jovanovich, 1988.

Hullfish, William, ed. *The Canaller's Songbook*. Long Beach: Bravo Productions, 1984.

Lamonte, Enid. *We Were There at the Opening of the Erie Canal*. New York: Grosset and Dunlap, 1958.

Phelan, Mary. *Waterway West: The Story of the Erie Canal*. New York: Thomas Y. Crowell, 1977.

BIBLIOGRAPHY - SECONDARY

Abbott, Jacob. *Marco Polo's Voyages & Travels on the Erie Canal*. Interlaken: Empire State Books, 1987.

Adams, Samuel Hopkins. *Chingo Smith of the Erie Canal*. New York: Random House, 1958.

Adams, Samuel Hopkins. *Grandfather Stories*. New York: Random House, 1955.

Chalmers, Harvey. *How the Irish Built the Erie*. New York: Bookman Associates, 1964.

Condon, George. *Stars in the Water: The Story of the Erie Canal*. Garden City: Doubleday, 1974.

Garrity, Richard. *Canal Boatman, My Life on the Upstate Waterway*. Syracuse: Syracuse University Press, 1977.

Wyld, Lionel. *Boaters and Broomsticks*. Utica: North Country Books, 1986.

Wyld, Lionel. *Low Bridge, Folklore and the Erie Canal*. Syracuse: Syracuse University Press, 1962.

Edmonds, Walter D. *Mostly Canallers*. Syracuse: Syracuse University Press, 1987.

Merrill, Arch. *The Towpath*. Rochester: The Gannett Company, Inc., 1945.

I WOULD LIKE YOU TO MEET SAL McMURRAY

I know she looks a little scary with that right eye that sends chills down your spine when she looks at you, and the missing tooth is a little disturbing, not to mention the way she brandishes that knife back and forth to make a point. And, yes, her clothes are shabby and in need of a good washing, but behind that surly disposition is a heart of gold.

Gretchen Murray Sepik takes us on a journey down the Erie Canal in the year 1830, where you will meet Crazy John, who runs around with his long johns on; and Wally the Wonderful, who is a mind reader. You will hear of the fight Sal had and how she lost her tooth, and wonderful stories about six-foot-tall frogs, tightrope walking mules, skunks, snakes, and dead bodies in the canal; and you just might learn a thing or two about the building of this engineering marvel.

GRETCHEN MURRAY SEPIK

is an actress, storyteller, playwright, and now author and illustrator. Her mother, Jinny, was a singer, and encouraged creative expression through dance, improvisation, and song. Her father, Michael, was a wonderful storyteller and dancer.

Gretchen is an actress with Young Audiences of Rochester and Young Audiences of Western New York in Buffalo, where she was honored in 2004 for her work with young people and her commitment to learning through the arts. She presents her characterizations of historical people, real and fictitious, in schools, universities, libraries, museums, historical societies, festivals, and more. She calls her form of acting, Experiential Theatre, because the audience becomes part of the program. "That child becomes my daughter, that one my son, that adult my sister," she said.

As Gene Tiesler, a teacher at West Irondequoit Rogers Middle School wrote, "You bring history alive in a way only a select few can do."

A student wrote, "You are the funniest person I ever met."

Regarding performances:

"...one of the absolute best speakers to address our Diversity Management members."

C.S., Staff, Attica Correctional Facility

"Trustees commented very favorably on the program and one gentleman told me it was the best program we have had in years."

M.B., NIOGA Library System

Gretchen says, “I love what I do.”

“It’s true!”